EDWARD
AND THE
PIRATES

EDWARD
AND THE
PIRATES

David McPhail

LITTLE, BROWN AND COMPANY

New York ❧ Boston

Little, Brown and Company

Hachette Book Group USA
237 Park Avenue, New York, NY 10017
Visit our Web site at www.lb-kids.com

First Edition: April 1997

Library of Congress Cataloging-in-Publication Data

McPhail, David.
    Edward and the pirates / David McPhail. — 1st ed.
        p.   cm.
    Sequel to: Santa's book of names.
    Summary: Once Edward has learned to read, books and his vivid imagination provide
him with great adventures.
    ISBN 978-0-316-56344-4
    [1. Books and reading — Fiction.   2. Imagination — Fiction.   3. Pirates — Fiction.]
I. Title.
PZ7.M2427Ef   1997
[E] — dc20   95-38451

10   9

IM

Printed in Singapore

The paintings in this book were done in acrylic on canvas.

Recipe for Edward:
Take one son (Tristian),
add one nephew (Patrick),
mix with love.
And this is for them.

And for all my friends at the Hope Town School,
especially for Bradley, prince of the pirates.

Once Edward learned to read, there was no stopping him.

Cereal boxes at the breakfast table...

seed catalogs that arrived
on the coldest day of winter,

the inscription on the monument in the town square,
and *books* — *all kinds* of books.

Edward especially liked stories of adventure. When he read about Admiral Peary racing by dogsled to the North Pole, Edward was right alongside, comforting the brave dogs and urging them on.

When he read that the bold outlaw Robin Hood was surrounded by the evil Sheriff of Nottingham's men, it was Edward who came to the rescue.

And when he read about Joan of Arc leading her troops to victory, it was Edward who carried her shield and held it up just in time to deflect the blow of a battle-ax.

Sometimes what Edward read seemed to become real. Once while he was reading a book about dinosaurs, he was convinced he'd seen a tyrannosaurus looking in his window.

Next to home, the library was Edward's favorite place.
He had his own library card and could borrow all the books he
could carry.

    One day Edward found a book lying on a shelf behind some
other books.

    The book was old and covered with dust.

    Edward blew away the dust and read the title:

Lost Pirate Treasure

    He sat down and began to read: "Some pirate treasure has
never been found...."

Edward was still reading when he felt someone tap him on the shoulder. It was Ms. Torres, the librarian. "Time to go, Edward," she said. "The library will be closing soon."

Edward checked out the book and walked home, arriving just in time for supper.

That night Edward went to bed early, taking his book with him. When the pirate ship was being tossed about on stormy seas, it was Edward who bravely took the helm. . . .

Sometime in the night, Edward felt his bed being bumped.

Edward sat up and looked around and saw he was surrounded by pirates!

"What are you pirates doing in my room!" he demanded.

"We've come for that book," answered the pirate who seemed to be the leader. "We think it tells where our treasure is buried."

"I can't give it to you," Edward explained. "It's checked out on *my* library card — you'll have to wait till I return it."

The pirates begged, but Edward wouldn't change his mind.
They pleaded, but Edward folded his arms around the book
and shook his head no.

They even promised him a share of the treasure — but that
didn't work either.

"You'll have to walk the plank!" threatened the pirates. But
Edward stood firm.

Finally one of the pirates drew his sword and waved it over Edward's head.

"Hand it over!" he roared.

But Edward wouldn't budge.

"Better be quiet," he warned the pirates, "or you'll wake up my mom and dad."

Edward had just finished speaking when the door to his room
burst open and someone riding a huge white horse charged in.
It was Edward's mother!

She was dressed in a shining suit of armor and was carrying a lance. She pinned the sword-waving pirate to the wall.

But then the other pirates drew *their* swords and closed in for the attack!

Suddenly a flurry of arrows flew through the air, knocking all the swords away.

A figure dressed in a green tunic bounded into the room, bow drawn, arrows at the ready.

It was Edward's father!

"Back off!" he commanded the pirates. "Go stand in the corner."

The pirates did as they were told.

"Don't hurt us," they begged.

Edward felt sorry for the pirates.

"They only came for this book," he explained to his mother and father. "I don't think they meant any harm."

Edward handed the book to the pirates.

The head pirate held it open while the others huddled close by, talking in whispers.

After a few minutes, the pirate gave the book back
to Edward.

"It's of no use to us," he said sadly. "We can't read."

"You can't read?" asked Edward.

"Not one word," answered the pirate. "None of us can."

"I'll read it to you, then," said Edward. "That is, if it's all right
with my mom and dad."

It was.

"But don't stay up too late," Edward's mother told him firmly.

"And close the window when you leave," said Edward's father
to the pirates.

As his mother and father left the room and went back to bed,
Edward opened the book and began to read aloud:
"'Some pirate treasure has never been found....'"